Peppa's BIG Feelings

Adapted by Lori C. Froeb

ISBN 978-1-339-04633-4

10 9 8 7 6 5 4 3 2 1   24 25 26 27 28

Printed in the U.S.A.   40

Licensed by:

First printing 2024

Book design by David Neuhaus

SCHOLASTIC INC.

Peppa and her friends have lots of happy times together. They smile and laugh and feel good. Sometimes, though, they may feel angry, worried, or sad. Those are big feelings.

Big feelings can be hard to understand, but they don't usually last long. There are even things you can do to help yourself feel better. Let's see what Peppa and her friends do!

Peppa is feeling angry. She thinks her tea party is ruined. What can make Peppa feel better?

Peppa finds a quiet spot in the clubhouse and takes time to cool down. She takes a slow, deep breath in. Then she counts to five as she slowly breathes out.

First, I breathe in . . .

. . . then out.
1, 2, 3, 4, 5.

Peppa, would you like more tea and some cookies, too?

Thank you, Granny.

After her breathing exercise, Peppa does not feel so angry anymore!

Poor Pedro is in the hospital with a broken leg. Pedro's mommy went home to get him some clothes and games. Pedro has never been in a hospital before.

There are lots of doctors and nurses rushing around. Pedro is feeling a little worried. What can he do to feel better?

Pedro tells the nurse how he is feeling. She talks to him and hands him his teddy bear. This makes Pedro feel better.

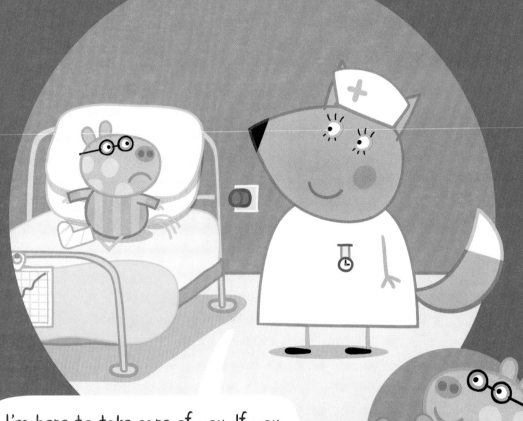

I'm here to take care of you. If you need anything, you can press this button and I will come to help.

Now Pedro is not so worried anymore!

Suzy and Peppa are having a great time playing in Suzy's bedroom. They play all afternoon, but then it is time for Peppa to go home. This makes Suzy want to cry.

I don't want Peppa to leave!

Suzy is feeling sad that her friend needs to leave. What can she do to feel better?

Suzy begins to cry a little and gives her mommy a big hug. Then Suzy remembers that she will see Peppa again very soon.

It's okay to feel sad when your friends leave. You will see Peppa again tomorrow.

See you at playgroup!

Suzy is not sad anymore. She can't wait to see Peppa tomorrow!

Tomorrow is not so far away!

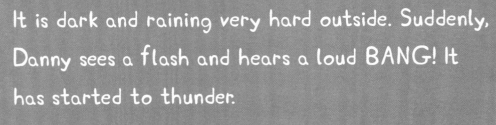

It is dark and raining very hard outside. Suddenly, Danny sees a flash and hears a loud BANG! It has started to thunder.

What was that sound? It was so loud and scary!

Danny is feeling a little scared. What can he do to feel better?

Danny holds his daddy's hand. Then he asks
his mommy to explain what the sound is.

I'm right here, Danny.

The sound is thunder. When
lightning heats up the air,
it makes a loud noise. It
sounds scary, but thunder
can't hurt you.

Now that Danny understands what the sound is,
he is not so scared anymore!

Thunder isn't so scary after all!

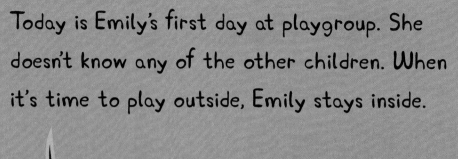

Today is Emily's first day at playgroup. She doesn't know any of the other children. When it's time to play outside, Emily stays inside.

I want to play with the other children, but I don't know what to say or do.

Emily is feeling shy. What could she do to make friends?

Emily uses dolls to practice asking a friend to play. She takes her time. When she feels brave enough, she asks Peppa to play.

Can I play with you?

Yes! Would you like to play my favorite game?

Emily is not feeling shy anymore, and she's made a new friend!

Everyone has big feelings sometimes. Can you remember a time that you've felt angry, worried, sad, scared, or shy? What did you do to feel better?

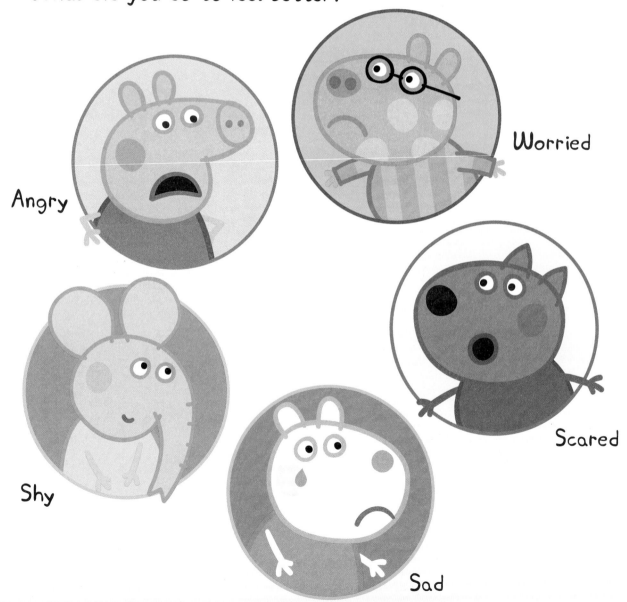

Angry

Worried

Shy

Sad

Scared